Diary of an
Angry Alex: Book 9

By **Crafty Nichole**

Contents

Contents

Day One Hundred and Thirty-Five

8:30am

An intervention. I still can't believe it. These idiots went out of their way to throw me an intervention for being angry? Well, whatever the case, Steve and Herobrine both went through their list of concerns. I guess I have been a bit angry lately. Or maybe always. I can't really remember a time when I wasn't angry.

Of course, being told that I'm angry by everyone I know when I'm not even angry, well, that's a great way to make me angry.

It doesn't matter. I don't have any more options. I'm currently on my way back to my old lairs. They told me that I have one chance to go through and pick up anything I think I might need, and then it's on to anger management.

Anger management. Ha! What does that even mean? I guess I'll find out as soon as I get packed.

10:00am

The ride to the old cabin wasn't as long as I remember it being. Bucky must be in a hurry to get rid of me. I guess I understand. I was kind of rude to him. And I chose to be Herobrine's apprentice even though Bucky never liked Herobrine. That wasn't great of me.

Anyway, there's nothing here at all. Nothing survived the attack. I already knew that though. I guess I just had to come back to check. It's been a long time since I've been happy. It might be worth it to give this whole "anger management" thing a shot.

Then again, there should still be something left over at the old nether lair.

2:00pm

That's more like it. It's a good thing those ghasts didn't actually blow up that TNT. Herobrine moved it, but not too far. It was in a chest in his room. Now, I have it safely tucked into my inventory, and no one has to know about it. It'll be my secret weapon, just in case this anger management thing doesn't really… manage my anger.

5:00pm

Well then. I get all the way back to my stupid spawn point and Steve and Herobrine are still arguing about

DIARY OF AN ANGRY ALEX: BOOK 9 – DAY ONE HUNDRED AND THIRTY-FIVE

what to do with me. Didn't they have that figured out before the stupid intervention?

The bottom line of it seems to be that Steve thinks I should go stay in some little village that'll help me find "inner peace" or something. Herobrine says that I should just go on a complete rampage, let everything inside of me out, kill a bunch of people, and burn stuff down until I feel better. Either way, it looks like I'll probably end up in that weird resort place. It sounds like a waste of time, but Steve and Herobrine won't shut up long enough for me to tell him to fall in a hole.

5:42pm

It took a while, but they came to a decision—all without me. Steve won the fight. It was a long one, let me tell you. But eventually, it came down to Bucky, Cloud, and Rudolph. They sided with Steve. Well, I mean, they can't talk exactly, but they lined up behind Steve. I knew that they didn't like Herobrine, but this is just ridiculous.

Well, I get it. I wasn't the best owner for them. Still, though. They don't have to make it personal.

It's been decided. I'll be going to some weird camp that will supposedly make me happier and less angry

3

and then everyone can just get off my back about everything. Steve says that it isn't supposed to be anything drastic, just enough for me to get a handle on my anger problem. Well it hasn't been a problem so far!

7:56pm

Bucky gave me a good kick to the gut and we're well on our way to the anger management place. I'd just like to say, for the record, that I am going to this place against my will and I don't think this is what I need. I might get angry sometimes, but it isn't like I'm always angry.

Except right now…I'm so mad. I'm incredibly angry. I'm furious! I'm livid! I don't need this! I'm perfectly happy! I'm so happy that my face is what they put on greeting cards! I've never been happier!

Oh wait, we're here now.

9:00pm

This place is…weird. It's one of the villages, but I haven't been here before. I had no idea it was out here. We rode for a short way past the lava jungle, and here we are. It's really well lit, easy to find. It's odd that I didn't find it before.

4

There's a wall around the village and a big gate leading in. Two iron golems are guarding it. I'm going to take a good look around before anyone wakes up.

And I should find somewhere to hide my TNT before it gets taken away. I'll find a good hiding place, one that no one will stumble across on accident. I'm positive that I have the smarts.

Look at that. Only a few minutes here and I'm already thinking positive! This therapy stuff is going to be a piece of cake!

9:30pm

It's done. I hid the TNT. It's down the well in the middle of town. Maybe it isn't original, but it worked just fine when I needed to dig that secret mine. That feels like it was forever ago.

I suppose the best thing to do is to find somewhere to get some sleep and have a good look around in the morning. There's something weird about this place, but that's no reason to miss out on a night of sleep. The gate is already shut, so it looks like I'm here to stay. At least for now.

5

Day One Hundred and Thirty-Six

10:30am

Wow, I'm glad I took the time to hide that TNT last night. First thing in the morning, one of the golems killed me so the good doctor could search through my stuff! At least he let me keep my diary. Apparently it's a good tool to organize my feelings. I can tell you how I'm feeling right now, and it's not very calm!

But I did get a chance to meet the doctor. His name is Dr. Testificate, and he's a jerk. How is killing me for no reason supposed to make me any less angry?!

Our first therapy session is going to be very soon, but I just had to get that off my chest. What a complete jerkface.

2:15pm

I'm not sure exactly how this therapy is supposed to help me, especially since the doctor is so infuriating. But, he explained the basics of how things are supposed to work. Every day, I'll have a task to complete. Nothing too difficult, just a bunch of things to lower my stress and anger. To be honest, it sounds terribly boring, but I guess that's the point, right? Bore me to death so that I don't get angry about stuff anymore.

Another part of the therapy is to keep up with this diary and use it to organize my feelings. That shouldn't be too hard. I talk about my feelings all the time…it's just that I usually only feel angry…

The last part of the therapy is to talk to Dr. Testificate about all my feelings, and I mean all of them. He wants me to go over the events of every day and figure out how things make me feel. I guess the point is to track exactly what makes me angry so that I can avoid them or fix them or something. I guess we'll see how things go today.

Today's task is pretty easy. And boring. I've got to plant a tree and make it grow. Shouldn't be too hard. I just need a sapling and some bone meal. There aren't any trees in the village though. Looks like I need to get the golems to let me out through the gate. Maybe I'll plant the tree in town. It would be nice to have an apple orchard again. The villagers might like it.

That's what I'll do! I'll go get a bunch of saplings and plant a nice little orchard. That should show that jerk doctor that I'm not just angry all the time.

4:00pm

It wasn't easy to find oak trees this close to the jungle. Plenty of jungle trees and even a few birches, but the oak trees took a bit of searching. And what do I find when I get to them? Skeletons. Perfect, right?

Wrong. I didn't have any of my weapons because the jerk doctor doesn't want me to hurt anyone. How am I supposed to get bones without killing any skeletons? Well, I couldn't get close enough to kill the skeleton anyway. I have a sapling, but no bone meal. What the heck am I supposed to do now?

7:00pm

I've just been staring at this stupid sapling and waiting for it to grow. And the whole time, the villagers have been wandering around with stupid looks on their stupid faces, honking in their irritating voices.

It doesn't matter. I've got to go back to Dr. Testificate and tell him that I couldn't grow the tree. I hate failing at life like this. I hate it!

How is this supposed to make me any less angry again?

9:30pm

I've had it with this day and this stupid place. Talking about my feelings only makes me angrier. The conversation with Dr. Jerkface went terribly. He didn't listen when I told him that I needed my weapons. Apparently, I should have just asked the farmers for some of their bone meal. Well, excuse me for trying to do what I was told! How was I supposed to know that the farmers have bone meal? Those lazy bums never do anything! The whole time I was out by the sapling, I didn't see anyone do anything that looked like work! They just wandered around and stared at me.

I hate this place. I'm tired and cranky and I don't want to do all of this again tomorrow.

Oh, it looks like Steve is here. I wonder what he wants…

10:00pm

Stupid jerk. He was just checking on me to make sure I didn't run away. Yeah, yeah. I get it. I'll give this place another chance. Whatever. I'm tired. It's time to go to bed.

Day One Hundred and Thirty-Seven

10:00am

The morning meeting with Dr. Testificate went okay,
I guess. Today, he let me pick what I wanted to do.
He gave me a short list of things I have to accomplish
over the next few days. All of them were pretty boring: tame an ocelot, go on a boat ride, make a new
friend, bake some bread, blah blah blah. None of it
seems terribly exciting, but maybe it'll be fun to go
and find an ocelot to tame. I haven't really spent too
much time in the jungle since Herobrine set it all on
fire.

At least I'm great at catching fish. That part should be
pretty easy.

12:15pm

I have more than enough fish for the ocelot, so I
cooked some up for myself. It's not the most exciting
lunch, but it'll give me the energy I need to climb
some trees. The rest of the fish, well…let's just say
that my pockets might never smell the same.

2:55pm

Just when I was about to give up, I found the perfect tree to climb. I'm going to make a chest and leave the few things I've got left down here. I don't want to fall down, die, and lose everything. It was a bit of a hike to get out here, and I'm positive it'll all despawn before I get back if it gets left lying around on the ground.

Oh! I think I see an ocelot up there! Fantastic! This day is looking up already.

3:02pm

Well…good news and bad news…

The good news is that I didn't die. The bad news is that the ocelot fell out of the tree and died.

The worse news is that I also fell out of the tree and just about broke my legs off. I can't really limp my way through to try to find another ocelot. Well, I guess there's some cocoa right here. It's better than nothing, I guess…

4:30pm

I'm back at the village now, and I've had the best idea! Why not take this tasty, tasty cocoa and bake some cookies? That should be a great way to make a friend. It'll be a good way to make something out of the day. It'd be better than wasting an entire day. Besides, I like baking cookies. It should be a great way to heal my wounds and calm myself down.

6:00pm

I'm on my way back to see Dr. Testificate now. I had the best idea ever: if I give some of the cookies to the doc, then he'll be the one to be my friend! Then he'll be nicer to me, and maybe he won't make me do so many idiotic tasks!

8:00pm

I'm so…UNBELIEVABLY ANGRY! Not only did the jerk doctor reject my extremely generous and friendly offer of fresh cookies, but he also gave me a lecture! He told me that I was wrong to give up on taming a cat just because I was "close to dying" and "worried about my shins."

This jerk tried to get me to apologize for not trying hard enough! After he went ahead and gave me a whole list of things to choose from! I shouldn't have said anything at all. I should have just stuffed the cookies in his stupid mouth and left.

He had the nerve to ask why I didn't have any milk to go with them! And he didn't even eat any! Not even a BITE!

I've had it. I can't be bothered. Why should I try anymore? None of this is worth the trouble. Why am I even here again? I doubt it's to fix anything about me. Maybe someone just wanted me to kill this horrible, awful doctor. THAT actually makes sense!

Hold on, one of the villagers just popped in to say that I have a visitor...

8:30pm

It was Bucky. Of everyone I know, I wasn't expecting to see him. Honestly, I thought he was mad at me. He brought me a couple of slices of melon. I guess that's his way of telling me to keep up the good work. It's actually rather sweet of him...

Okay. I'll let go of everything and give this place another chance. "Tomorrow's another day." At least, that's what Dr. Jerkface always says. One more chance, and then I'll figure out what to do about this terrible place.

13

Day One Hundred and Thirty-Eight

9:30am

I still have that checklist of things to take care of. Since I messed up on the whole "taming an ocelot" thing, maybe I'll go on a boat ride today. There's a river nearby that should be peaceful enough. I'll find a boat or craft one or something before I go in to see Dr. Jerkinson.

9:35am

You'll never guess what finally happened. That's right. My tree finally decided to grow. Lazy jerk tree. Well, at least I've got the wood to make myself a boat. I'll store the rest of it in my little cabin in case I need it later. I got two saplings from the leaves as well. I'll go ahead and plant them for later. Wood is always useful, and I still haven't given up on making another orchard.

Just listen to me. Too much longer here and I'll start getting ready to live here forever. I need to figure out how to get out as soon as possible. I don't want to turn into another one of these mindless villagers.

10:40am

Okay. I've checked in with the idiot doctor and I'm about to set off towards the river. It's well to the east, so I'll get a good amount of exercise. Man do I wish that I had Rudolph or Bucky or even Cloud with me. I guess a nice stroll will help with the relaxation of it all.

12:15pm

At least it would be relaxing if it wasn't for all of the TERRIBLE CREEPERS IN MY WAY! STOP BLOWING ME UP ALREADY! FALL IN A HOLE AND ROT THERE!

2:00pm

Maybe the doctor isn't completely stupid. The gentle rocking of the boat, the warm sun on my face... This isn't so bad. I should do this more often. I think I've reached the coast. Yes, yes I'm drifting out to sea. That's fine. I don't much care where I end up. Anywhere is better than that terrible compound.

2:35pm

I've definitely been drifting for a while. I wish I had my fishing rod with me. It's strange to think of how much I hated fishing when it was something that I had to do. Now, it seems like a wonderful pastime.

2:50pm

It looks like I'm coming up on a marshy kind of biome. I don't think I've been out this far before. I wonder if there are witches out here. It might not be so bad, you know?

Oh dear, I do seem to be getting quite hungry though. I should think about turning back soon.

3:00pm

Oh no…

8:00pm

What a day. A terrible day. How can things go so downhill so fast? No, not downhill. Freaking underwater! I was much hungrier than I thought I was. I ended up slamming my boat into a lily pad of all things. A lily pad! What kind of joke is that? A lily pad that can smash a boat. Ridiculous.

It wouldn't have been so bad if I'd had some food with me. I didn't realize until it was too late, and I ended up starving to death so very, very far away from the village. I grabbed some food from the villagers and sprinted back to where I died. I was so tense and worried and nervous, and when I finally got to the spot, I splashed around for so long looking for my things.

It turns out that another of my "friends" had dropped by to help me out: Herobrine! He'd been keeping track of me, watching from a distance. He saw me smash my boat, and then starve to death. Instead of being a huge jerk like I thought he would, he had actually picked up my things and held on to them for me.

Well, the only thing I really had was my diary, but he saved it for me! Herobrine giving me a hand; I never would have guessed. But he actually helped me out.

I think that these friends of mine actually do want me to get better. I mean, this place is such a terrible way to do that, but they really do mean well.

Anyway, that's what I was thinking. I explained things the best that I could so that Herobrine could understand how awful things have been in therapy. It didn't take all that much convincing. I guess that's not much of a surprise—living with just Steve was irritating enough for both of us, so living in a whole brainwashed village of "nice people" is so much worse.

He understands me. I know he's on the same page as me. Before he left to go back to whatever it is that he's doing, he gave me a flint and steel. He must have been back to the nether recently and noticed that I took all of the TNT out from where he hid it.

I'll stash the flint and steel with the TNT beneath the well on my way back into town.

10:30pm

After getting back to town (and safely storing the flint and steel in my hiding place), I was way too tired to get yelled at for dying in the dumbest possible way. So I lied. I know that's the wrong way to do therapy, but I'm just so tired of all of this.

Maybe that's the point of all this "therapy." To make me so tired that I can't be angry anymore.

Or maybe I should have just been lying all along. It made the therapy session go much easier, and I didn't get lectured or yelled at. I even kind of like making up stories about nice, peaceful days out and about in the world.

Mostly though, I just want to get out of here as soon as possible. I'm not any less angry than I usually am. I don't like getting lectured for stuff that isn't my fault, and more than anything else, I'm super tired of people telling me what to do all the time.

Maybe that's what I need: someone that I can give orders to for a while, since everyone else seems glad to order me around. That's something I might really like.

Day One Hundred and Thirty-Nine

10:20am

I'm standing outside of town with a shovel and a plan. Well, my task for today is to plant a flower in a pot. I'll have to go digging for clay, and if I know this stupid jerk doctor at all by now, I won't be able to get away with giving him just any stupid flower. No, I'll search all over and find him the nicest freaking flower on this whole entire map.

But that's not what my plan is. See, I have another plan. A bigger plan. One might call it evil, but I call this whole stinking place evil. And I'm going to blow it up.

Don't worry. I'm not angry about anything. I mean, I'm plenty angry about plenty of things, but that's not why I'm going to blow up this nice little resort. This home away from home. This tiny freaking slice of heaven! No, it's going to be the newest crater in the area because Dr. Jerry "Jerkface" Testificate is the actual worst villager that ever existed, and I've gotten rid of a lot of villagers for a lot less. He needs to be exploded into the biggest hole and then buried there.

But I can't be the one to do it. No, see, it's the same if I were to run away. If I just "give up" on my therapy, Bucky or Steve will just drag me back here or find someplace even more awful and I'll be stuck. They're the ones that decided they want to be my friends. They threw that awful intervention, and now they're the ones keeping me stuck here.

So to get out, I'll need to convince Steve that explosions are the only way to solve this. And to do that, I need to find him.

12:45pm

There's still no sign of Steve in any of the areas directly around the village. Herobrine might be keeping a close eye on me, but it looks like Steve was less interested in watching me plant trees and bake cookies. Figures.

Well, maybe Herobrine just likes to see me suffer. That makes more sense.

I have the clay that I need for the flowerpot. I'll swing by the old village and see if Steve's over there. It's close enough, and there's a big field nearby that should have some nice flowers.

4:15pm

It wasn't quite in the plains area, but I found a lovely bit of lilac in the forest near the village. I didn't get a chance to go inside the village though. Apparently they're still a little mad about the whole "attacking them" and "trying to burn everything down" thing that I did when I was working with Herobrine. Well, that's just…

Sigh

It's kind of awful, isn't it? I did some pretty rotten stuff before. I guess I understand why they wouldn't want to let me back in.

But they could at least tell me where Steve is! All they would tell me is that he isn't here and "He better not come back." Apparently we've both been banished from the village forever.

I wonder how hard it would be to craft an invisibility potion…They can't keep me out if they don't know I'm there.

4:25pm

On second thought, I'm pretty sure I need fermented spider eyes to get potions of invisibility. Yuck.

4:29pm

I mean, spider eyes are already gross and a pain to get, but actually fermenting them? That's just disgusting!

4:37pm

Yes, I realize I'm just stalling so that I don't have to go back to see Dr. Jerkface, but can you blame me?

Okay. Time to go back.

Long sigh

7:30pm

As expected, he didn't like the lilac. Apparently his favorite flower is allium. Who even cares? I did exactly what he said, and it still isn't good enough.

He says that tomorrow I have to do better if I ever want to get out of this place. Of course I want to get out! I can't figure out why these other idiot villagers are staying here! Is there something in the well water besides my TNT?

10:15pm

Just as I was getting ready for bed, you'll never guess who turned up…It was Steve! He was checking up on me again. Perfect timing! I've never been so glad to see Steve in my entire life.

Well, come to think of it, I've never been glad to see Steve at all. But this almost evens things out.

I spent a while talking to him about the way things have been going here. I can tell that he doesn't believe me, but he's agreed to stick around for a while. After my morning session with the jerk doctor, I'll take him around and show him all of the things that have been going wrong for me over the past few days.

Maybe it'll be enough to convince him to help me.

Day One Hundred and Forty

9:30am

This is it! Today's the day that I turn all of this around. I'll go and get my task of the day from the idiot doctor, and then I'll bring Steve with me, wherever Dr. Jerkface tells me to go.

11:00am

Ah, perfect! So today, the doc gave me the same checklist as before and told me to "actually finish something on it this time." I know, what a JERK!

But it doesn't matter. One of those things on the list was "make a friend." Since I have Steve with me now, I can take him with me and finally have something done right. But until then, I should give Steve the grand tour...

2:30pm

I can't believe it. Nothing! I took Steve through and showed him all of the horrible things in this stupid village—the derpy villagers, the stupid jerk trees that grew where I had to grow the first jerk tree, the river of death, the horrible jungle that's half buried in lava and half on fire.

To be fair, I guess he already knew about the lava jungle.

But the rest of it! No reaction! Nothing! I can't believe I expected him to believe me and actually take my side. I don't know why I ever could have been so trusting. Steve isn't a great friend, but I'm still going to bring him to Dr. Testificate and pretend that he is. Maybe after one of our therapy sessions, Steve will finally understand how terrible all of this really is.

7:30pm

Is any of this real? Have I fallen into some kind of alternate reality? I don't know exactly what has been going on, but while Steve was there, the jerk doctor was on his best behavior. I mean, he wasn't a jerk at all! He didn't say anything rude or mean. He didn't even insult my intelligence!

He did tell me that I didn't do the task right, since Steve was "already my friend." It didn't matter how much I protested, he completely shut me down. Why bother arguing at all? I'm getting used to always being wrong. I'm so frustrated and tired and all of this is such a bother.

But at least Steve offered to stay with me for a few days, just until he was sure that I was really settling in okay.

Maybe the jerk doctor was right about something for once. Maybe Steve was my friend all along.

10:20pm

Steve, you stupid idiot jerk, those were my LAST COOKIES! He's not a friend. He's nothing like a friend. Friends are supposed to be generous and kind and NOT COMPLETE JERKS!

FALL IN A HOLE. I HOPE IT'S THE LAST HOLE YOU EVER FALL IN: YOUR GRAVE.

Day One Hundred and Forty-One

8:25am

I'm willing to forgive Steve for constantly stuffing his face with my cookies since he's still going with me for my therapy today. I told him not to come to the morning session today so that I can choose an appropriate task.

None of the tasks have ever seemed hard, but there's always a catch to them, always something that I don't expect to go wrong. I wonder what that'll be today.

9:45am

No list today. I think the doctor is getting bored with letting me pick out what I want to do. Instead, he told me that I have to grow my own wheat and bake it into bread. I'd say that sounds like an easy enough task, but look how hard it was just to grow a stupid tree.

No, I'm going to get Steve and have him help me with this. Maybe then he'll see just how worthless this whole anger management thing is.

12:00pm

So far, it doesn't seem like things are too out of control. Since I have to grow my own wheat, I asked the farmer to let me use some of his farmland. He agreed without any kind of a fuss. I'm waiting to see where the hard part will come in.

12:15pm

Humph. I wanted to just steal some of the farmer's seeds to use, but no, Steve wouldn't let me. He said that it was cheating to steal and that I needed to do everything fair and square. So now we're about to head out of the village to find some grass to cut down. If I'd known that Steve was going to be this much trouble, I would have just toughened up and finished this stupid therapy by myself!

1:00pm

No, I was wrong. Steve had the right idea. Also, Steve brought a sword. He easily killed a few of the skeletons that seem to always hide out in the forest during the day, so now there's plenty of bone meal to grow the wheat. I tried to tell him that Dr. Jerkface wouldn't let me have my weapons or I would have done that myself, but I don't think he believed me.

And he told me to stop calling Dr. Jerkface a jerkface. What was the point of coming to help me if he's just going to order me around some more? Is that supposed to make me less angry? Is it Steve?

Oh, right. I have a task to get back to. I have the seeds, and Steve gave me the bone meal. It looks like we're about to grow some wheat and bake some bread.

2:45pm

I can hardly believe it. The bread is baking now, and nothing terrible happened. There wasn't even anything slightly inconvenient! This is fantastic!

3:00pm

No, wait, this is terrible! How am I supposed to convince Steve that all of this was just a big waste of time if things keep going so smoothly?

Maybe Dr. Jerkface will shout at me when we bring him the bread. Maybe he wanted rye or pumpernickel or something fancy like that. There's absolutely no way that he'll just take the bread and say that I did a good job.

30

7:00pm

I fail at life. A lot. I can't believe this. He didn't like the bread...he LOVED it. I think I might be having a heart attack. I'm so angry that I can actually hear the blood being pumped through my body. What is this? Why now? How come whenever Steve's around, everything just works out fine? Why do I fail at life so badly?

And that's not the worst part. No, the worst part was after the session. The jerk doctor told me to stay back and talk to him alone for a second. I don't know exactly what he saw, but I think he could tell that I was mad about the whole bread thing. I tried to pretend that everything was normal and I was perfectly happy and all, but he could definitely tell that something wasn't right.

He told me that he doesn't know what I'm up to, "But I know you're up to something." How freaking scary is that? Why does he have to make it sound so much like a threat?

Oh, I was wrong. That wasn't the worst part. The actual worst part was when I tried to talk to Steve about it, but he said that I was probably just overreacting. Overreacting? I'll show you overreacting, you stupid whiny jerk!

Okay. Right. I'm calm. I'm fine. Getting angry isn't going to convince anyone that I'm ready to leave this place. I'll just do a little bit of deep breathing…count to ten…okay. All better.

But if that jerk doctor thinks he can just threaten me and get away with it, he can fall in a deep dark hole!

Day One Hundred and Forty-Two

8:00am

It was hard getting to sleep last night. I kept thinking about what Dr. Testificate said. If he knows I'm "up to something" or whatever, how much else does he know? Does he know that Herobrine came to see me?

Does he know about the TNT in the well? What if he found it and took it away? I want to go and check to see if it's still there, but I can't do that during the daytime. Someone will see me go down there for sure, and I can't trust anyone in this awful place. Not even Steve.

Not yet, anyway. I'm bringing him with me today and keeping him nearby, no matter what happens. He's got to see everything the same way that I do. Otherwise, I'll never be able to convince him that everything here is just the worst.

9:45am

The jerk doctor was suspicious that I brought Steve to our morning session, but there's no getting around that now. He already knows that something's wrong, so it doesn't really matter if he doesn't want Steve around. I want Steve around...wow that felt weird to say. But it's true, and it's my therapy. I should be able to do it however I want.

The task for today is pretty simple. I just have to make a painting of something beautiful. I already have the wood for the frame, so I just need to get my hands on some wool. After that, well, it's easy to craft a painting. What could possibly go wrong?

I can only hope that something goes very wrong. If not, Steve will never be on my side and get me out of this whole therapy nightmare.

10:25am

We have a few supplies to take a nice, leisurely walk and get some wool. I had to borrow some iron from the blacksmith to make some shears. The blacksmith had to watch me craft it to make sure I wasn't making anything dangerous. I knew the jerk doctor had the villagers spying on me! I'm not angry though. It just helps to prove my case: everything here is weird and I just want to leave.

Steve didn't think it was weird at all. He seemed surprised that I haven't already tried to make my own weapons and go on a huge killing spree. It's good to see that I have such good friends who think so highly of me...NOT. Thanks for nothing, Steve.

Our walk to the plains takes us pretty close to the lava jungle. Maybe Steve would like to go for a little swim...

1:25pm

So I didn't shove him in the lava lake. I was so tempted, but it wouldn't help us get through today's task

We're eating a late lunch of mutton. Yes, we had shears, but it was so nice to just kill something for once. And it's been too long since I've had a good bit of meat. Cookies and bread can only get me so far.

Well, that and the potatoes that I stole out of the farm and baked up in the blacksmith's furnace. What? It's not like the farmer was doing any farming! He's even trading emeralds for people to bring him the wheat out of his fields! And I replanted all the potatoes I took!

But we're about to head back to the village. I have everything I need to make a painting. I wish that things hadn't gone so smoothly. I think Steve is even more convinced that this place is helping me. Maybe I shouldn't be so nice to him.

4:00pm

On the way back, I did try to punch Steve into the lava. He was pretty mad, but he didn't fall in. I need to work on my aim. I've gotten so out of practice with my fighting skills while I've been here. It's only been a few days, but I feel so worn out.

But the painting is made! I put it up on a wall and sure enough, it took a few tries to get a good one. But a lovely sunset picture seems like the perfect thing to turn in for this stupid assignment.

Oh, this gives me an idea…

8:00pm

Well, that was a disaster. My idea worked, though. Instead of bringing the jerk doctor to see the painting, I took the painting to him. Sure enough, instead of a lovely sunset, when I put up the painting, it showed this huge picture of a skull on fire; it was the opposite of whatever pretty, peaceful thing he wanted.

That's even what he said. He lectured me about what the difference was between a pretty picture and a scary one. Man, if he thinks that skull is scary, he obviously hasn't ever been to the nether. Or seen Herobrine when he loses his temper.

So I listened to this stupid lecture, and afterwards had to listen to Steve tell me that the doctor was right. What a joke. How could he still not get how lame this place is? It isn't helping, and I've been here for a week!

I told Steve that I've been doing my best and the stupid jerk doctor isn't doing anything except making me angrier. I'm tired of him not listening to me. He hasn't seen what happens when I actually fail at a task, though. And it'll be hard to fail tomorrow's task. "Climb a mountain and build a snow golem." What a joke.

I'm thinking that it'll have to be something extreme to finally make Steve understand just how terrible things have been here.

And there's only one person I know that really knows the meaning of the word "extreme." He should be around here somewhere…

11:25pm

I found Herobrine lurking around the outskirts of the village, just on the other side of the wall. We have a plan that should make sure that Steve sees the doctor's bad side for real.

It's going to involve spiders. A LOT of spiders.

Well, hopefully Herobrine will actually help me out. So far, he's been a better friend than Steve. At least Herobrine actually believes me. Heck, he even listens better than so-called "good guy" Steve does.

But then again, at least Steve is here for me right now. He hasn't given up on trying to help me, no matter what.

I *guess* they're both pretty good friends, even if Herobrine is a scary dude who snores too loud and likes to drop anvils on my head, and Steve is a selfish jerk who likes to boss me around and eat all my cookies.

Whatever. It'll work out fine. It has to. I'm out of options at this point.

Day One Hundred and Forty-Three

8:00am

Today's the day! It was hard getting to sleep knowing that I'm so close to getting out of here. The plan for the day is really simple. It's impossible to screw it up!

Escape Plan:

1. Check in with Dr. Jerkface.

2. Get up the mountain with Steve.

3. Spend some time playing in the snow. Don't let Steve know that anything is strange.

4. Get down to business building the snow golem.

5. Herobrine unleashes his spiders; we can't fight since I don't have any weapons.

6. Flee back down the mountain and return to Dr. Jerkface.

7. Listen to his stupid jerk lecture.

8. Get Steve on my side.

9. Blow up the village.

That should be all it takes for Steve to realize that things here are too terrible to let me stay. If nothing else, it'll show him that I haven't been making things up just so I can get out of therapy.

Oh, he's waking up! It's time to go and put the plan into motion!

11:30am

Things are going fine. Steve and I have just finished a great snowball fight! I guess I forgot just how much fun we used to have together. It doesn't matter. I'll be out of here soon, and then we can have however much fun we want.

We just split up to try to find a pumpkin to make the golem. I'll let him look all he wants. I need to find Herobrine and tell him that everything's in place for him to let the spiders loose.

11:42am

It's all set up. As soon as Steve gets back, the spiders will attack. They won't kill us...probably...

1:25pm

Hahahaha, the spiders totally killed us. Completely. I thought Herobrine would have told them not to, but he didn't. It's okay though; I'm not mad about it. Not even a little! Herobrine even brought my diary back to me and left it in my cabin. He really thought everything through to help me the best that he could.

Steve, well…he's over in the corner, shouting his head off. He's so mad! He gets it! He finally understands that this is what I go through every single day!

He wants to go and talk to the jerk doctor about it and explain why we couldn't finish the task. I'm so incredibly…happy? I am! I'm so glad! He's finally going to understand why I've been so frustrated!

I'm going to finally see one of my plans through to the end!

5:00pm

HAHAHAAA HAHA HA HEEHAAWWWW!!!

It's been such a long time since I let out a good evil laugh! But it's happening! For real! My plan is working!

The doctor gave us both a lecture about "keeping your word" and "seeing a task through to the very end," but Steve wouldn't listen at all! He kept trying to explain that it would be stupid to climb back up the mountain if there were just going to be spiders all over the place to kill us again.

Steve was still mad when we left the doctor's, so I talked to him again about getting out of here. And he listened! He really listened to me!

I took it a step further and told him about the TNT. It was a big leap of faith, but Steve didn't think it was a bad idea! He told me to wait for a while, to let him think about it.

I'm a little nervous that he might have some second thoughts about all of this, but I can give him until nightfall until I try talking to him again. It's a big decision, I know, but turning this horrible place into a huge crater is really the only option left.

I can only hope that Steve agrees with me.

7:00pm

He hasn't tried talking to me about the plan yet. I'm starting to get really worried. Maybe I moved too soon. He might not be ready for such drastic measures.

Oh, he's coming this way! Maybe I spoke too soon!

10:00pm

After a very difficult conversation, I finally got through to Steve. No matter what I've said before, he's a good friend.

His only real worry was that I would take things too far. He agrees that the doctor is a big problem, especially if other people ever come here in the future looking for help. Instead of letting me go blowing up everything, Steve insisted on being the one to do it.

I don't know why, but that makes me so much happier. He cares about my recovery and doesn't want me to go out and kill anyone out of revenge, but he still agrees that we need to take care of this here and now.

I gave him the TNT out of the well, and he's wiring up the redstone now. He said that he's going to make two explosions: one in the doctor's bedroom while he's asleep, and one in the wall to give us a way out. Herobrine and I are waiting over by the wall—a safe distance away—ready to make a break for it the second we see Steve running over.

Bucky, Cloud, and Rudolph are waiting for us on the other side of the wall, ready to take us anywhere we want to go after we escape. Well, Rudolph is still the only one that will let Herobrine ride him, but I don't mind riding Bucky for now. Cloud seems to like Steve well enough anyway. I guess we just need to figure out where we want to go…

Ah! I just heard the first explosion!

Day One Hundred and Forty-Four

5:00am

The sun still isn't up, but I can't sleep. I mean, I don't have a bed, so of course I can't sleep, but even if I did, I don't think I'd be able to sleep. We've been riding for some time now.

It's still hard to believe that Steve went through with it and blew up the doctor's office! I mean, I can't really prove that Dr. Testificate is gone, but I can only trust that Steve went through with it. He says so, and friends have to trust each other, right?

The animals are getting tired. I'm not really sure where we're headed, but I do know that it's going to be a whole new experience.

I can't really speak for the other two, but I can't think of any reason that we can't all try to live together again. It didn't really work out before, but things have really changed since then. Steve and Herobrine both showed me that they can be my friends, and I think they have a newfound respect for each other. Steve likes that Herobrine helped me out when no one else would, and Herobrine likes that Steve wasn't afraid to blow some stuff up and cause real mayhem.

Things could really work out. For the first time in a long time, I have real hope that things are going to get better. Hahahaha. Maybe all of that therapy really did help me out.

To be continued...

Made in the USA
Coppell, TX
09 December 2024

42077454R00030